琵琶甲虫

高洪波◎著　　画儿晴天◎绘

谭旭东 · 周利娟◎译

海峡出版发行集团
THE STRAITS PUBLISHING & DISTRIBUTING GROUP
福建少年儿童出版社

图书在版编目（ＣＩＰ）数据

琵琶甲虫：汉英对照/高洪波著；谭旭东译. —福
州：福建少年儿童出版社，2010.3
（高洪波童诗绘本系列）
ISBN 978 - 7 - 5395 - 3562 - 3

Ⅰ．琵…　Ⅱ．①高…　②谭…　Ⅲ．①英语—汉语—对照读
物②儿童文学—诗歌—作品集—中国—当代　Ⅳ．
H319.4：I

中国版本图书馆 CIP 数据核字（2009）第 160993 号

琵琶甲虫
——高洪波童诗绘本系列

作者:高洪波
出版发行:海峡出版发行集团
　　　　　福建少年儿童出版社
http://www.fjcp.com　　e - mail：fcph@fjcp.com
社址:福州市东水路 76 号（邮编：350001）
经销:福建新华发行（集团）有限责任公司
印刷:福州德安彩色印刷有限公司
地址:福州市金山浦上工业区标准厂房 B 区 42 幢
开本:889 × 1194 毫米　1/12
印张:2.5
版次:2010 年 3 月第 1 版
印次:2010 年 3 月第 1 次印刷
ISBN 978 - 7 - 5395 - 3562 - 3
定价:20.00 元

高洪波

简介 ABOUT THE AUTHOR

高洪波，笔名向川。儿童文学作家，诗人，散文家。1951年12月出生，内蒙古开鲁县人。中共党员。鲁迅文学院七期、北京大学首届作家班毕业生。1969年应征入伍。转业后曾任《文艺报》新闻部副主任、中国作家协会办公厅副主任、《中国作家》副主编、《诗刊》主编、中国作协创联部主任、中华文学基金会理事长。现任中国作协党组成员、副主席、书记处书记，《诗刊》主编，中国作协儿童文学委员会主任。

1971年开始发表作品，1984年加入作家协会。先后出版过《大象法官》《鹅鹅鹅》《吃石头的鳄鱼》《喊泉的秘密》《我喜欢你，狐狸》等14部儿童诗集；《波斯猫》《醉界》《人生趣谈》《高洪波军旅散文选》《墨趣与砚韵》等30余部散文随笔集；《鸟石的秘密》《渔灯》《遇见不不兔》等11部幼儿童话；《鹅背驮着的童话——中外儿童文学管窥》《说给缪斯的情话》两部评论集以及诗集《心帆》《诗歌的荣光》等。2003年7月，中国少年儿童出版社出版了《高洪波儿童文学文集》。曾获过全国优秀儿童文学奖、"五个一工程奖"、国家图书奖、庄重文文学奖、冰心奖、陈伯吹奖、中国少儿出版社"金作家"等奖项。

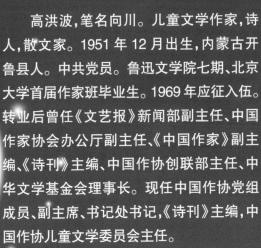

今年我突然想起自己当年在腾格里沙漠遇到的一种小甲虫，感到非把它写成一首童话诗不可，于是开始酝酿、构思。童话诗不好写，一需故事二需诗，可是我写得有几分轻松和随便，主要是小甲虫首先感动了我，事实上是它领着我走出沙漠的。

每个人都有一个心灵的沙漠。

愿这只小琵琶甲虫属于你。

——作　者

Inscription

A beetle that I met several years ago in Tengeli desert suddenly occurred to me this year. I felt I must write the fairy poem about it, so I began brewing the idea. Fairy poems are hard to write because they need both story and poem. But I wrote a bit freely and casually, mainly because the little beetle touched me, and also because it was in fact it who led me out of the desert.

Each person has a spiritual desert.

I would like this little beetle to belong to you.

零伍

一

腾格里,腾格里
天上掉下来的奇迹

——民谣

莽莽的黄沙如海,　　　　一望无际的黄沙,

漫漫的沙丘似山;　　　　一望无尽的苍凉,

山的沉默,　　　　　　　一望无垠的沙丘,

海的威严,　　　　　　　一望无边的哀伤,

装饰得腾格里　　　　　　由一只忙碌的小甲虫驮着,

神秘又静寂,　　　　　　匆匆忙忙　走进

冷峻又遥远。　　　　　　无涯的岁月,

　　　　　　　　　　　　直到今天　爬入

　　　　　　　　　　　　我的诗行。

那是美丽的王昭君
出嫁塞外的一刻，
当她幽怨的目光
再也望不见思念的家乡，
怀中的琵琶被风沙
一阵拍打 指尖儿
竟拨不出一丝音响，
于是王昭君愤然一掷，
马蹄"的的" 昭君远去，
只留下沾有她体温的琵琶
黯然神伤……

琵琶的躯体和灵魂
在岁月的风暴中粉碎，
将清冷的声韵
在腾格里大漠中贮藏。
当琵琶消失的那一个时刻，
有无数梨木色的甲虫
开始繁衍于沙漠，
游走成诗意盎然的小生命
——琵琶甲虫
　　名声响亮。

活脱脱是一群
袖珍型的琵琶，
椭圆的身体是半梨状音箱，
昂起的头颅如弯曲的琴弦，
细且尖锐的足爪
像琵琶的弦柱，
只是忘却了王昭君的乡愁，
每日里在沙砾间觅食，
再不肯弹拨江南的向往。

故事的主人公
是一只平凡的小甲虫，
他在静寂里出生
　静默中长大，
天生的小哑巴
枉称为小琵琶，
因为发不出一丝声音，
他感到命运有些古怪，
自己有必要
走出这个静谧的童话。

月亮跌入沙漠
溅起一汪清泉
——民谣

小琵琶在大漠上穿行，
他滑动的身影
被朝阳拉长，
成为一叶小船的模样。
沙漠的早晨清凉如水，
是甲虫们锻炼的好时光，
小琵琶跑起甲虫马拉松，
月牙泉水在脑海荡漾。
传说在大漠的尽头
有一湾蓝色的泉水，

那是王昭君弹琵琶的象牙拨子
被风暴夺走，
从此琵琶甲虫们
才永远沉默不语。
失去了明丽的歌唱，
琵琶的美妙音响
全在那月牙泉里珍藏。
找到它，
沙漠会由黄转绿，
水草将肥美异常，

甲虫们不再为一茎枯草争执，
还将拥有红色的花朵
粉色的芳香
绿色的湿润
紫色的歌唱。
一种爱飞翔的亲戚
——蜜蜂和蝴蝶，
也会欣然前来拜访，
翅膀上闪动着太阳的光芒。

小琵琶就这样离开洞穴，
决心到月牙泉去踏访，
背回弹响琵琶的拨子，
为琵琶甲虫的种族，
也为了自己
　　未曾拥有的昂扬。

沙丘很大，
甲虫很小，
小甲虫在大沙丘上
用尖细的足爪拨动沙砾。
调皮的沙砾纷纷流散，
逃避着小甲虫的攫捉。
微弱与强大抗争，
一寸一寸。
大漠似在退却，
屈服于一个甲虫的意志，
小琵琶，走向远方……

树是沙漠的旗
　　　　　——民谣

远方有一株老树
半边枯黄半边嫩绿，
如静止的油画般
站成倔强的象征，
向小甲虫发出生命的呼唤。
那偶一摆动的嫩枝
遥远中显示亲近，
叶片上闪闪烁烁。
望一眼老树，小琵琶
身上便涌起异样的感觉：
树下可是月牙泉，
那神妙的象牙拨子，
可曾遗落在疏朗的树荫？

昏黄的落日隐入昏黄，

炎热正渐渐消退，

沙丘下有寒意升起，

小甲虫与老树

仍在遥遥相对，

感觉不到自己的速度

真是最大的伤悲。

他终于攀上了又一座沙丘，
老树在月光下招手，
月亮挂在它的枝丫间，
像卡在巢间的鹰蛋。
这轮腾格里的月亮
奇妙又圆润，
像祖先在月中凝望自己，
一种久远的共鸣
在体内轰然响动。

月亮啊月亮，
古树上的月亮，
腾格里的月亮，
银白如玉的月亮，
真想奔向你的殿堂，
去分享你的纯净透明，
去体味你的玉质珠光，
去寻找祖先遗落的音韵，
让琵琶甲虫的种族
　　恢复叮咚的歌唱……

与月亮对视的刹那，
小琵琶的灵魂感到轻松欢畅。
他发现自己僵硬的翅膀
颤动出飞翔的欲望，
向前耸身一跃，
月色陡然明朗，
前方的古树与明月，
幻化成灿烂的太阳……

月亮弯弯，
升上树巅，
小琵琶睁开眼，
才发现自己睡得好甜，
一个绮丽的飞翔梦，
一支壮美的甲虫曲，
鼓舞他继续攀援……

九曲黄河万里沙

——民谣

不知跨过了多少沙砾，
不知流掉了多少热汗，
（如果甲虫也有汗腺）
老树终于立在眼前。
小甲虫伏下身体
贴紧温暖的大地，
仿佛有隐隐的雷声
在他心里积郁。

摇动着嫩绿的枝条，
老树发出邀请，
请他爬上树冠
做一次高空游览。

与行走沙漠的感觉相反，
小琵琶感到步履矫健，
尖细的爪下如有风生，
翅膀也愉快地震颤。

步步登高，
步步望远，
哦　树下是别一种景观——
一条黄色的大河
正在脚下流过，
发出澎湃的涛声，
挟裹着无上威严。
细细倾听，
大河涛声
有春天生命的呼唤，
有夏天炽热的情感，
有秋天快乐的恬静，
唯独没有冬天的冷淡……

大河涛声滚滚，
大河浪花拍岸，
凝望这雄浑的长龙，
小甲虫
忘记了寻找的月牙泉。
这条流动的黄绸带啊，
系住了一个沙漠甲虫的心弦，
激起了他的全部情感，
陡然忆起那绮丽的梦境。
于是他向大河纵身一跳，
天空里划过一条
　　细微而醒目的
　　　　梨木色的闪电。

辽阔的空间，
短暂的时间，
小甲虫从树巅
向黄河里飞翔。
他的足爪划破空气，
翅膀扇出嗡然锐响，
琵琶的音韵铿锵滚动。
遥远的古曲
　　灿烂辉煌，
离别与聚首的感觉，
欢乐与幽怨的交织，
还有大漠的歌声与叹息，
月亮的嘱托和希冀，
一齐在这飞动的甲虫身上
　　悠然共鸣。

高傲的百灵鸟们
也停止了歌唱，
向小小的琵琶甲虫
投以羡慕的目光。
黄河轰然大笑，
以浊天的巨浪
迎接一个纤小伟大的生命，
小甲虫随黄河远去，
远去的黄河神采飞扬。

五

沙漠，不可破译的谜

——作者自题

腾格里沙漠很大，
很大的沙漠
有着亘古的沉寂，
很大的沙漠
有悲伤也有欢乐，
一只甲虫的失踪
竟会使大漠抽泣。

这些都是大漠的秘密，
破译它的只有大漠居民：
那些忙碌的甲虫，
匆匆的蜥蜴；
那些冷静的锦蛇，
　　热情的沙鸡。
伟大的腾格里身上
印着一只小甲虫的足迹，
线一样通向远方，
风沙的手不肯抹去，
真诚的腾格里
要贮存这珍贵的记忆。

当我们再一次望见月亮
　　望见沙丘上的古树，
当我们又一次听见涛声
　　听见春天里的小雨，
小琵琶都会适时出现，
以一只小甲虫的固执
小甲虫的谦虚，
告诉我们奇特的经历，
从寻找和追求开始，
以献身和投入结束，
一次平凡又非凡的际遇。

小琵琶，小生灵
我要向你致敬，
——当然，要经过你的允许
不为别的，只为了
你那琵琶梦幻的无比绚丽
和以生命弹拨的那支
大漠琵琶曲……

One

Tenggeli, Tenggeli,

the miracle down from the sky.

—from a ballad

The sand is vast as sea,

The endless sand dunes are like mountains.

The silence of the mountains,

The majesty of the sea,

Decorated Tenggeli.

Mysterious and silent,

Solemn and remote.

The endless sand,

The endless desolation,

The endless dunes,

The endless sadness,

Carried by a little busy beetle,

Hurried in boundless years.

Until today, climbed into

My verse.

It was the moment,

When the ancient beauty Wang Zhaojun

Married beyond the Great Wall,

When her eyes with hidden bitterness

Could no longer see her home,

The lute (pi-pa) in her arms flapped by the sandy wind.

Her fingertips could no longer play a hint of sound.

So angry, Wang Zhaojun threw it away,

Then she left with her horse's clip-clop,

Only leaving the depressed lute (pi-pa)

Warm with her body temperature,

The lute (Pi-pa)'s body and soul

Smashed through years of storm,

The desert buried its rhythem as well.

The moment when the pi-pa disappeared,

Countless pear-colored beetles

Began multiplying in the desert,

Incarnating themselves into poetic little lives,

—with a resounding fame of Pi-pa beetles.

The pi-pa beetle

Is really a mini lute.

Their oval body is a loud speaker in the shape of a half pear;

When raised, their heads are like bending strings;

The claws are fine and sharp as the strings of pi-pa.

They forgot Wang Zhaojun's nostalgia.

Every day they seek food in the gravel,

Never think of the South.

The hero of this story was a small, ordinary beetle.

He was born in silence,

Grew in silence.

A born little dumb,

Undeserving the name "pi-pa",

Unable to utter even a slightest sound,

He felt his fate weird, and should

Get out of this quiet fairy-tale.

Two

The Moon falls into the desert,
Splashing into a clear spring

— from a ballad

The small pi-pa walked through the desert.

His shadow was elongated,

By the morning sunlight,

Resembling a small boat.

The morning in desert was as cool as water,

It is a good time for beetles to exercise.

The small pi-pa ran a marathon,

The water in Crescent Moon Spring waved in its mind.

It was said that at the end of the desert,

There was a blue spring.

That was Wang Zhaojun's ivory plectrum of her lute,

Which was taken away by the storm.

Since then, the pi-pa beetles lost their crisp singing, and

Were silent forever.

All the pi-pa's wonderful sound,

Were collected in the Crescent Moon Spring.

If you found it,

The desert would turn green;

Grass would be luscious,

Water clear

The beetles would no longer fight for a withered blade of grass;

They would also have red flowers,

Pink fragrance,

Green moisture,

Purple singing.

Their relatives who love flying

—bees and butterflies

Would be pleased to come for a visit,

Wings reflecting sunlight.

The small pi-pa left his cave,

Determined to find the Crescent Moon Spring,

To carry back the plectrum,

For the pi-pa beetle's race;

As well as for a spirited sound,

Which he had never owned.

The dunes were very large;

The beetle was very small.

On large sand dunes,

The little beetle scratched the sand with his claws

The naughty sand all flew away.

To escape being captured by the little beetle.

It was resistance between the weak and the strong.

Inch by inch,

The desert seemed to succumb to the will of the beetle, and

Gradually retreated.

The small pi-pa, went to the distance…

Three

Trees are the flags in desert.

—from a ballad

There was an old tree standing in the distance,
Half of it was turning brown, just
Like a static oil painting.
It is a symbol of unbending character.
Giving life call to the little beetle,
Through occasionally swinging branches,
Distant but close.
The leaves sparkled

A look at the old tree,
The pi-pa got a strange feeling.
Whether the Crescent Moon Spring was under the tree?
Whether the marvelous ivory plectrum
Had been left in the shade of the tree?

The sun fell dim;
The heat gradually faded away;
Cold air was rising from the bottom of the dunes;
The little beetle and the tree
Were still a long distance apart.
Sad for him
Not be able to feel himself moving.

He finally climbed up to another sand dune.
The tree was waving at him in the moonlight;
The Moon hanging in its branches;
Like the eagle egg in the nest.
The moon in Tenggeli,
Wonderful and round,
As if an ancestor was gazing at him,
An ancient resonance rang out inside.

Moon, Ah moon
Moon in the old tree.
Moon in Tenggeli,
Silver as jade.

How I wish rushing to your palace,
To share your purity and transparence,
To feel your jade pearl,
To quest for the spirited sound of the ancestors,
So that the pi-pa beetle's race
could resume their crisp singing.

The moment when looking into the moon,
The little beetle's spirit felt eased and mischievous.
He found his rigid wings,
Vibrating with a desire to fly.
He leaped forward,
And the moonlight suddenly became bright.
In his front, old trees and the moon
Changed into the brilliant sun…

The falcate moon rose,
On the top of the tree.
The little beetle opened his eyes,
And found himself sleeping very deeply and sweetly.
A beautiful flying dream,
A magnificent beetle song,
Encouraged him to continue climbing.

Four

Nobody knew how many grains of sand he had climbed across;

Nobody knew how much sweat he had shed;

(If the beetles had sweat glands)

The old tree finally stood in front of him.

The little beetle bent closely.

Over the warm earth,

As if a faint flow of thunder,

Gathered in his heart.

Shaking its verdant branches,

The old tree sent his invitation to the visitor:

Climb to the tree crown,

Enjoy a high-altitude tour!

Totally different from the feeling of walking in the desert,

The little beetle was walking vigorously.

As if the wind was under his thin claws,

And wings happily quivered.

Nine bends of the Yellow River, ten thousand miles of sand.

—from a ballad

Ascending step by step,

Looking farther and farther into the distance,

Oh, under the tree is another landscape—

A yellow river flowing at the foot of the tree,

With swishing of the water and supreme majesty,

He listened carefully.

The sound from the waves,

Calling the life of the spring;

Displaying the emotion of the hot summer;

Possessing the quietness of the happy autumn;

Only excluding the winter's coldness,

The great river's waves were rolling and rolling;

The great river's waves were spraying banks.

Staring at the long and forceful river,

The little beetle forgot to

Search for the Crescent Moon Spring.

Oh, this flowing yellow river,

Fastened the heartstrings of a beetle in a desert,

Inspiring all his emotion.

He suddenly recalled his beautiful dream, so

He jumped off the tree toward the river.

Sailing across the sky,

A subtle but eye-catching,

Pear-colored lightning.

Through a vast space,

In a flash of time,

The little beetle flew

from the tree summit to the Yellow River.

His claws scratched the air;

His wings fanned with buzzing sound;

The pi-pa's temperament was rolling sonorously

The distant ancient classical music

was so brilliant.

The feeling of gathering and parting,

The interaction of joy and bitterness,

And the desert's songs and sigh,

The moon's instuctions and wish,

All resounded in the flying beetle.

The proud larks

Stopped singing, and

Cast envious eyes

To the little pi-pa beetle.

The Yellow River burst into laughter,

To welcome this tiny but great life.

With muddy waves,

The little beetle floated away with the Yellow River,

And the Yellow River flowed with high spirit.

Five

Tenggeli Desert is a great
Great desert,
With silence from time immemorial;
A great desert,
Has not only sadness but also fun;
The disappearance of a beetle
Could make the desert sob.

These are the secrets of the desert.
And only the local residents are able to interpret.
The busy beetles,
The hurried lizards,
The cool snakes,
                And warmhearted sand chickens.
On the body of the great Tenggeli,
Marked with footprints of a little beetle,
Leading into the distance like a line,
Which the sandstorm refused to erase,
Sincere Tenggeli
Wanted to store these precious memories.

The desert, a mystery we can never interpret.

—by the poet

When we gaze at the moon again, and
        the old trees on the sand dunes;
When we listen to the waves again, and
        the spring rain,
The little pi-pa will appear in time,
With his persistence and humility,
Telling us that marvelous experience, which
Began with quest and persuit,
Ended with dedication and commitment.
What an extraordinary but ordinary fate.

Little pi-pa, a small creature
I salute you, if
With your permission.
Only for
Your incomparable and magnificent pi-pa
And the desert pi-pa life melody…

读
《琵琶甲虫》

谭旭东

《琵琶甲虫》这首诗,你可以把它当作童话诗来读,也可以把它当作一般的生命诗来品读。你看,在诗人的笔下,那只腾格里沙漠里的琵琶甲虫,是多么富有生命力,是多么充满力量,多么给人昂扬的精神!《琵琶甲虫》发表后很受好评,《新华文摘》都给予了转载。要知道,在当代诗人中,高洪波的诗作是被《新华文摘》转载得最多的,只不过他从来不爱炫耀自己的诗歌成就!

《琵琶甲虫》缘于诗人一次沙漠里的旅行。他在腾格里沙漠看见了有无数梨木色的甲虫,它们顽强地生存并爬行于沙漠,让诗人的心灵深受震撼,于是他在多次酝酿之后,写下了这首童话诗。细细品读,你一定会发现琵琶甲虫的确是一个令人难忘的形象——它在荒漠里移动着黝黑的身体,整日四处奔波,用小小的足爪,匆忙而快乐地挖掘着生活。诗人看到它,产生了很多的联想,他想到了它是静谧的童话里的主人;他想到了小甲虫到月牙泉的拜访;他想到了小甲虫在月夜里,睡在老树下做了飞翔的梦;他想到了小甲虫朝黄河纵身一跳而发出的铿锵音律;他想到了昭君公主,想到了她出塞的琵琶曲;他想到了很多大漠的秘密——那只有理解了大漠居民,才能探索出生命真谛的秘密!

读这首富有音乐美的诗,我们分明感受到了诗歌内在的节奏。他的内心的情感是随着小甲虫的顽强的旅行而波动的,他对这个小小生命的钦佩,他对这个小小生命的敬重,既是对大自然生命的敬畏,也是对一种人格力量的崇拜。看得出来,诗人崇尚那种执著坚定的精神,追求那种在平凡中显示伟大力量的境界;看得出来,诗人是怀着不平静的心讲述一只小甲虫的故事的,他的笔下的小甲虫已经不是一只小甲虫,而是一个英雄形象——只不过它是一个无名英雄,一个在大漠里很不起眼的英雄!这个英雄没有像我们生活中的英雄一样做出舍己救人的好事,但它给予了诗人生命的力量,让读者感受了一种希望和阳光。

沙漠里有很多难以破译的秘密,但诗人以这首童话诗破译了一个沙漠里的秘密,破译了一个沙漠里生命的秘密,向我们解读了一个倔强的生命所具有的力量与美!

在诗的题记里,诗人有两句话:

每个人都有一个心灵的沙漠。

愿这只小琵琶甲虫属于你。

这两句话,就是对《琵琶甲虫》这首的主题的一个很诗意的诠释。对呀,每一个人都有一个心灵的沙漠,但如果走出这片心灵的沙漠,就需要有小琵琶甲虫那种力量与精神!因此读懂了《琵琶甲虫》,就等于读懂了人生之路。人生之路有很多艰难险阻,会遇到很多挫折坎坷,但只要你坚定信心,富有顽强拼搏的意识,并且能够脚踏实地,你就能够战胜一切,成为真正的强者!

《琵琶甲虫》里的小甲虫给我们弹奏了一曲感人至深的生命之歌!